Ohio Thunder

by **Denise Dowling Mortensen**

Illustrated by **Kate Kiesler**

Clarion Books
New York

Clarion Books
a Houghton Mifflin Company imprint
215 Park Avenue South, New York, NY 10003
Text copyright © 2006 by Denise Dowling Mortensen
Illustrations copyright © 2006 by Kate Kiesler

The illustrations for this book were executed in oil paint.
The text was set in 18-point Meridien Medium.

www.houghtonmifflinbooks.com

Printed in Malaysia

Library of Congress Cataloging-in-Publication Data

Mortensen, Denise Dowling.
Ohio thunder / by Denise Dowling Mortensen ; illustrated by Kate Kiesler.
p. cm.
Summary: A powerful thunderstorm sweeps across an Ohio farm.
ISBN 0-618-59542-2
[1. Thunderstorms—Fiction. 2. Farm life—Ohio—Fiction. 3. Ohio—Fiction. 4. Stories in rhyme.] I. Kiesler, Kate, ill. II. Title.
PZ8.3.M842Oh 2006
[E] —dc22   2005002107

ISBN-13: 978-0-618-59542-6
ISBN-10: 0-618-59542-2

TWP 10 9 8 7 6 5 4 3 2 1

To Scott, for all the roads we've traveled together
—D.D.M.

For Pa Kiesler, who taught me to count the
seconds between thunderclap and lightning bolt
—K.K.

Hazy heat,
sweaty brow.
Dusty field,
tractor plow.

Dark horizon,
speckled sky.
Cornstalks rustle,
blackbirds fly.

Soaring, growing
anvil form.
Locomotive,
charging storm.

Eerie calm,
tractor crawl.
Bright red roof,
thick black wall.

ZAP!
One hundred million volts.
Cloud to ground
advancing bolts.

Ohio thunder,
Rumble, Boom!
Cold front coming,
coming soon.

Downdraft gust.
Heartland churn.
Tractor humming,
safe return.

Nanosecond
lightning FLASH!
One one-thousand—
thunder CRASH!

Wild wind blowing.
Nature's brew.
Locomotive passing through.
Thundering 'cross
Ohio plains,
bringing waves
of quenching rains.

Marble hail
pelting crops.
Goosebump shiver,
icy drops.

Downpour slowing,
clouds run dry.
Lightning flickers,
brightening sky.

Scented earth,
swaying trees.
Screen door creaking,
gentle breeze.

Blackbirds squawking.
Sunlight streams.
Summer's bounty
glistens, gleams.

Ohio thunder,
rainbow bloom.
Harvest coming,
coming
soon.